The M⊙th Keeper

Also by K. O'Neill

The Tea Dragon Society
The Tea Dragon Festival
The Tea Dragon Tapestry
Princess Princess Ever After
Aquicorn Cove
Dewdrop

The Moth Keeper

K. O'Neill

RH GRAPHIC

NEW YORK

The Moth Keeper was created on an iPad Pro with Procreate.

Copyright © 2023 by K. O'Neill

All rights reserved. Published in the United States by RH Graphic, an imprint of Random House Children's Books, a division of Penguin Random House LLC, New York.

RH Graphic with the book design is a trademark of Penguin Random House LLC.

Visit us on the web! RHKidsGraphic.com • @RHKidsGraphic

Educators and librarians, for a variety of teaching tools, visit us at RHTeachersLibrarians.com

Library of Congress Cataloging-in-Publication Data is available upon request.
ISBN 978-0-593-18227-7 (hardcover) — ISBN 978-0-593-18226-0 (paperback)
ISBN 978-0-593-18228-4 (library binding) — ISBN 978-0-593-18229-1 (ebook)

Designed by Patrick Crotty

MANUFACTURED IN CHINA
10 9 8 7 6 5 4 3 2 1
First Edition

RH GRAPHIC

A comic on every bookshelf.

For Alex

Chapter One

Then one night, a young quail lost track of time, and hurried home to the village, long after the sun had set.

The sigh of an eerie night-wind reached his ears, along with the sound of raindrops. Surprised, he looked up at the sky.

The Moon-Spirit was crying.

They soon discovered that the desert at night was very cool and peaceful, with a quiet splendor of its own.

To thank the villagers for their kindness in joining her at night, the Moon-Spirit offered a special gift—her enchanted Moon-Moths.

She taught the villagers how to care for the Moths so that they would pollinate a special tree called the Night-Flower once a year.

From this tree they would receive gifts and blessings to make their life by night easier.

In time, other folks who were enchanted by the stories of life beneath the stars came from across the land to join the nocturnal community.

Then I vow to do my best to guide you on your path to becoming our new Moth Keeper.

The ceremony was lovely, Anya.

Thanks, Estell! I've worried for days that the Moths might not follow me instead of Yeolen...

I think they'd follow anyone who smells like pollen puffs.

Speaking of which...

Guess who made 'em on her own for the first time today!

Wow! Nice one!

cough cough

I think I can handle this.

phwooo

Chapter Two

It's cozy when I do this!

You look like a wee Moth grub wrapped snug in its cocoon.

If it gets any chillier, we'll leave the Moths in the nest for a night or two.

If the Moths are cooped up for too long, their power will begin to fade after a time.

Magic's a wild thing. It only flows when life is left to exist in its own natural way.

A bit of preserved spice root inside the mouthpiece warms up the breath as you play.

Saves frozen fingers on nights like these!

I'm no bard by nature, but no one can hear you tootling away out here while you get the hang of it.

Thank you, Yeolen. Did you make it?

I carved the ocarina, but Aimoss is the one who knows the secrets to preserving spice root so that it stays extra peppery...

I think...
it's done?

What do you
think, Healer
Aimoss...?

Would you feel confident giving this to your first patient?

Maybe...

...not.

In fact, it is as good as any of us would have made.

We all have days when we can't quite remember the ratio of things.

Or times when we feel unsure of our skill.

But with this...

This will help her through the snows.

I wish we could add pollen to everything.

I'm sure those who tend the silkworms and glowworms, and grow the plants we eat, wish for the same.

The pollen's magic is like roots, spreading throughout our way of life.

Without strong roots, our village would be worn down like stone in a sandstorm.

...What happens if we run out of pollen?

We wait for the Night-Flower to bloom again.

It is the longest night, after all.

45

46

Just at that moment, the moon shone brightly through the clouds—and a huge golden moon it was.

The girl stopped short, suddenly breathless.

The basket she had been carrying slipped and fell to the ground.

She ceased to feel her little brother's weight against her back.

She became utterly entranced by the beauty of the moon before her.

From that night onward, it was as if her spirit had flown across the vast sky and tied itself to the moon...

...leaving only her body grounded on the earth.

Each night, she felt herself grow small and withdrawn as the moon waned...

...and when it grew full again, her heart became so full she felt it might burst.

Many nights passed in this way.

Even at the moon's peak, she was filled with an indescribable sadness, knowing it could only last a night before it would begin to shrink again.

Her soul was trapped breathing in and out with the moon.

She thought of nothing but the moon.

50

After a time,
she no longer
noticed those
around her.

She began to fade into a half-existence, trapped on earth forever by her obsession.

To this day, she wanders. I have heard that her form is most clear during the full moon.

So you'd best be careful little creatures, or she may draw you under the spell of the moon, too!

Chapter Three

To be honest, Anya, it's been tough to find someone willing to take on the Moth Keeper job.

I can well understand—most folks can't imagine spending so long away from their loved ones.

Since my mentor passed, it's only been me. And before me, it was only her.

Could you tell me more about her?

Hm? About Yura?

Well, she was very wise, and very patient. Took her time to trust me an inch with the Moths.

See, at your age, I was a bit of a ruffian.

Yes...she helped me once. I was too shy to speak to her again afterward...then it was too late.

Hm...

Yeah, as a kid I was always on edge, mistrustful.

Pushed others away before they got a chance to do the same.

I didn't want to be a part of the village.

I couldn't understand why everyone didn't just fend for themselves.

Then I met someone who truly had reason to be mistrustful, yet he gave freely and openly, believing that it would be returned.

By that stage, the villagers had their doubts about me— fair enough.

But for the first time in my life, I wanted to try giving something, not caring if it was noticed or returned.

Of course, my mentor was no fool.

She made me prove myself over and over before she let me have any responsibility with the Moths.

Gradually, the other villagers saw that I was helping in my own way.

So now, Anya, what about you?

What drew you to a role so few are willing to choose?

I knew...that it would be hard at times.

But I thought doing this job—so important to our village—would keep me warm inside even on long, cold nights.

61

I suppose I've gotten used to being alone...

We live our lives surrounded by the darkness.

...I want to try to be a light for others.

It's all right if you don't feel ready yet, but how would you like to try handling a few nights of your own from time to time?

Tonight I learned how to make these.

Herb snacks for energy! You're already out by yourself so often.

Thank you, Estell. I feel all right, though.

The Moths are good company. They remind me why I'm out there.

I've been learning about how the Night-Flower pollen spreads.

It's amazing!

I used to think the pollen was a gift just for us, but so many things rely on it throughout the desert.

That's the magic of it—it's part of the rhythm of nature. Everything is connected.

You're always good at things like this.

She says she's fine...

But I think Anya put a lot of weight on her own shoulders.

She's taking it very seriously, but it's a long time to suddenly spend alone.

I'll keep taking more nights while she gets used to the solitude.

Thanks, Estell.

You seem to have a strong intuition for Anya's feelings.

Have you known her for a long time?

PHEW!

My, aren't you busybodies today!

This should keep you happy.

Another flower that I'll never see in full bloom...

If my
lantern went
out right
now...

...would I
even exist
anymore?

POF

Chapter Four

How does it sound to you, Madame Jaellara?

Tree language is complex and quiet.

It seems tired from the harsh winter, but I sense a good pulse of sap inside.

I believe it is doing fine.

Did life in the sun-village also revolve around a tree?

Not so much. Cacti were more valuable, storing cool water inside.

In our folktales, a wandering hero's life was often saved when a cactus grew miraculously out of the sand before their eyes.

I have not collected many sun-stories!

Someday you must tell me them, so I can add them to our library.

Healer Aimoss, when did you live in the sun-village?

I was born there.

Naturally, being albino meant that life beneath the sun was rather challenging for me.

My vision is better by daylight, but I rarely left the shade for fear of the sun's harsh rays.

Rather than a life spent chasing refuge in the shade, my parents decided to bring me to the night-village.

I haven't seen them in a while.

Do you remember what life was like in the sun-village?

...

I wonder...

Your mama said not to play too close to the entrances...

This is the only place these plants grow!

I need to make notes—they could have some use we don't know about yet.

Thank goodness...

...I forget how fragile you are.

You're so small.

And the night...is so big.

What is it, Estell?

I think...Anya is getting worn out.

It might...it might be good for her to stay in the village for a night or two.

I see.

Of course, I'll take over for a while.

Thanks for keeping an eye out, Estell.

Good evening, Anya!

Good evening!

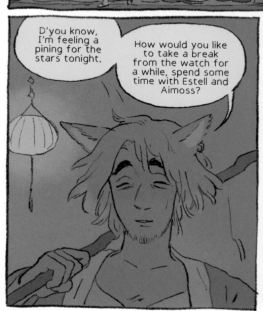

D'you know, I'm feeling a pining for the stars tonight.

How would you like to take a break from the watch for a while, spend some time with Estell and Aimoss?

Thank you, Yeolen. But I'm doing fine!

The Moths are easy, really.

123

Chapter Five

Anya, let go
of my scarf,
please.

I can't see the lights of the village, Mama...

I don't want to go any farther.

The wind is telling us to go home.

Please don't be so childish, Anya.

Let's just go on a little more, then we can sit and rest.

I don't want to!

There now.

Let's get these scampy Moths to bed. Then I'll bring you home.

Might take a little while, but we've got our lamp here to keep us company.

Just for a day, I want to know how it feels...

Pardon me, but I don't believe I've seen you around before.

It's a ritual every year.

This plant bursts into flower and attracts all manner of insects from across the desert.

Some of them are real delicacies, so there's always a friendly contest to catch the tastiest ones.

Sounds fun!

You're welcome to give it a try.

DA DUM!! DA- DA DUM!! Dum DUM- DA DUM DA

DUM DA DA DA!! D- DU

DA- DUM DA-DUM!! DUM-D DUM! DA! DA

This cactus flesh is very cooling.

Yeolen!

Chapter Six

CLATTER

182

Chapter Seven

I thought you might be heading out... I gathered a few things to help, if you need your strength back.

...

Thanks, Estell.

I don't know where to begin...

...but I know
they're out there,
somewhere.

You...!

...This Moth...

...feels like the moon.

Yes...it was a gift from the Moon-Spirit.

All this time I've tried not to look past the light of my lantern...

...but when I do, I can see familiar shapes even in the deepest shadows.

I smell a fragrance on the wind... like incense.

Is that the scent of the Moths?

Can you smell it, too?

Pardon me. I should have asked earlier.

What is your name?

Chapter Eight

Dawn is coming, and the Moths are a long way from home.

We'd better hurry...

Just one more...

If we don't find it now, it will be lost for good...

Can you sense it anywhere?

218

I have watched this little one's steps across the sand for a very long time.

It would have only caused pain to take her to the stars before her heart was ready.

Thank you for helping her.

Thank you, for the gift of the Moths.

Our village has treasured them...

But...

Chapter Nine

This light is strange...almost like an eclipse?

We heard a party and couldn't resist coming to see.

You're all usually fast asleep by now!

Look!

Estell...
Thanks for
packing the
Moth food.

At times it feels like there is a vast desert inside my head...

...As I walk across the sands, trying to reach something I think I need, the more lost I become.

THE END

INSPIRATION

Although Aotearoa New Zealand doesn't have what you'd typically think of as a desert, the high alpine regions around the Tongariro National Park and Kā Tiritiri o te Moana (Southern Alps) are very dry, covered with beautiful tussock fields and stony scree slopes. I was inspired by the rolling, undulating landforms, the lines of the mountain ranges, the colors of the receding distance, and the smallness one feels standing amid such scenery. Not far from my hometown, the dark sky reserve at Lake Tekapo, with its ocean of stars, also served as inspiration for this book.

Aotearoa, being made up of small islands isolated from other continents for millions and millions of years, has endless examples of highly specialized relationships between flora and fauna—plants and creatures that require one another to survive. There is a species of native moth that will only lay its larvae in a type of rush plant found in just a handful of wetland areas.

An example from the United States is the Joshua tree and the yucca moth. The Joshua tree flowers save their energy by producing only a small amount of pollen, which the moths have evolved to be able to carefully harvest and spread to other flowers. In the process, they lay batches of eggs inside that will eventually hatch and feast upon some of the pollinated seeds.

visible
stitching

lots
of
patch
work

layers